NO ONE IS COMING BACK

the forgotten war, shall be remembered

MANUEL PELAEZ

SCRIPTOR HOUSE
THE EPITOME OF GREATNESS

Scriptor House LLC

2810 N Church St Wilmington, Delaware, 19802

www.scriptorhouse.com

Phone: +1302-205-2043

Published by Scriptor House LLC

Paperback ISBN: 979-8-88692-237-0

eBook ISBN: 979-8-88692-238-7

NO ONE IS COMING BACK

the forgotten war, shall be remembered

MANUEL PELAEZ

Even though, many countries entered the war this is strictly a Korean story, on June 25, 1950, it was a cold windy day, the fog covered the ground and skies, light rain, it was miserable to be outside. This is when the first line of fire occurred. Scenes from hell came straight to us, there was so much confusion and indoctrinated hatred. We had no choice but to start a war with our own brothers and sisters. It was artillery shelling and explosions everywhere, so much destruction, there was no time to talk only engage in the madness of war. 815 thousand fatalities, this doesn't even consider the millions of civilians killed or forced to flee from their homes.

Throughout the years my people have been indoctrinated to hate each other like a sweet poison taking over our minds and souls. The memories of, The Chosin Reservoir, The Battle of the Imjin River, The Battle of Chosin, haunt me every single day. My name is Lee Hong, Lieutenant Colonel of a brigade that fought in the Korean War. When people talk about hell, this is definitely the closest thing to it on earth. It was brutal, we were one of many battalions fighting in this inferno. My eyes see the hell that took place on December 6, 1950 at the Chosin Reservoir. As for as the eyes can see forty nine divisions, nineteen brigades, 560, 000 troops. 5,350 tanks, 11, 337 artillery systems. 7032 missile defense systems, 13,000 infantry support systems. Equipment of the ROK army includes the older M47, M48. Newer K1 and K1A1 hosting a 120mm smoothbore gun. Newer XK2 Black Panther fitted with German MTV 1500hp europower pack engine. 120mm main gun optional 140mm smoothbore main barrel, new tanks equipped with radar equipment all-bearing and reactive laser detection armor.

I asked myself countless of times, why on hell do we have to kill our own brothers and sisters. Once this hell started there was no stopping it, this just continued to get worse. I couldn't sleep at night because of all the nightmares, I constantly prayed for this hell to end. Our battalion barely survived this conflict. So many fellow soldiers and close friends died in this hell. There's no time to show emotions because it will get you killed. So many explosions, death and destruction everywhere. Can anyone ever recover from seeing this everyday. It makes you think why can't we get along with our own kind which we all share the same Peninsula.

So many field army corps, divisions, brigades, battalions, company's, platoons, squads. Once this hell starts, you can't think only kill. It was one hell after another on December 6, 1950 at the Chosin Reservoir. All hell broke loose, so much firepower, death and destruction everywhere. The battle was endless and fierce, it makes everyone insane knowing why on earth is this actually happening. There's no time to think, either kill or be killed.

This continued day and night, the madness of war is completely insane. So many loses on both sides, so such suffering, the explosions are everywhere. Each side are firing back and forth, the dead are piled up everywhere. Who can get out of this alive, if anyone does they will never be the same after witnessing this hell. This is only getting worse, no sleep, no thoughts, only fighting to survive. Why, does humanity fall for this, what is the point of killing our brothers and sisters. 7,304 killed, 21,366 combat causalities, in addition, 30,732 none-combat casualties were attributed to the harsh winter and lack of food. Our battalion barely escaped this inferno, knowing this will be endless and even more brutal ahead. We must prepare ourselves for death which is always accompanied us like a shadow that never goes away.

These confrontations are what hell is truly like. On January 4, 1951, Seoul is recaptured. We had no choice but to retreat. We were heavily outnumbered and if we would have stayed our entire battalion and many more soldiers would all have perished. We will regroup and comeback even stronger, we will comeback because we fight until death. This time we were outnumbered badly and caught by surprised, but make no mistake this is far from over.

On April 25, 1951, our battalion wouldn't be so lucky. In the Battles of Kapyong Imjin River, is a day that my battalion will remember forever. Three days of hell, April 22-25, 1951. The bloodiest engagements, the memories of Hill 235. The brigade had lost a quarter of its strength suffering 1,091 casualties. Including 622 of the Glosters, the South Koreans 8,000, the loses on both sides were straight out of nightmares. On this day my entire battalion died and many more battalions also. We fought hard to the bitter end, it was an overwhelming inferno of firepower and explosions from everywhere. When death comes to you, it is very quick and decisive, it silences everything.

All your thoughts are gone, your breath halts. In a strange way a silent peace, they must be a purpose for everything. Now, I must continue telling this story from the other side. We did not die in vain, I am so proud of all the men that died on this dreadful day. Our brigade was hit hard, outnumbered by many foes, we stood our ground. We did not retreat, we were hit with an overwhelming amount of artillery shells, missiles, ground forces infantries. We all died like true soldiers, now after death I have permission to continue this story from the other side. Here everything is different, things like war, hatred, separation of countries and differences are none existent.

I will begin with my story, then I will talk to fellow soldiers in my battalion, other battalions and even the so called enemies which don't exist here. Even though, I can't get to everyone because the numbers are to great. One must remember that in this war there were 1.9 million causalities, including

815 thousand fatalities. Now, everyone will get a different perspective on what all the soldiers really think of killing their own brothers and sisters.

My name is Lieutenant Colonel Lee Hong (male) leader of the battalion. I was killed along with my entire battalion fighting endlessly. Out numbered badly, we were exchanging firepower when out of nowhere. Missile strikes, artillery fire 120mm, an enormous infantry ground forces.

The explosions were everywhere, direct hits. It was quick and lights out, I prefer that, but rest assured no cowards in my group. I leave behind my beloved wife Ara Hong. We were together for many years and our two daughters Sena and Nari Hong. We live in the city of Itaewon in South Korea. I can only hope that my girls can grow up in my love from far away. I will try my best to comfort them and my beloved wife. My sister Chin Sun, bless her heart, and brother Gwon, I miss them so much, and my parents I will miss endlessly. One by one my battalion will tell their stories so our deaths will be remembered. Now, it's Major Bak Choi (male), we stood our ground but we were overwhelmed. As my tears fall from my face, I leave behind my wife Min Choi, our baby son Nam Choi. I am the only child, my beautiful parents who I love so much. We live in Dong Daer Un in South Korea, I will try my best to comfort them from far away. I will watch over them, my memories are with them. Captain Chu Mae (male), we stood our ground until the very end, in one moment I saw my arm ripped away from my body. The explosions finished us off, it was quick and I saw my fellow soldiers die proudly with me on the battlefield. Now, I will try my best to keep it together as the tears fall from my face. I leave behind my other half and purpose for happiness. My wife Moon Chu, our beautiful children daughter Byeol and son Won. They are both so active in their school and hobbies. My parents who are very supportive will help out my wife. My brother Heo, who has always admired me as I rose in the ranks. We live in the city of Samseongdong in South Korea. I will try my best to comfort them and watch over them. Medical Staff Areum Kim (female), we gave medical assistance in the field of battle to exhaustion, but in the end we were outnumbered badly. My heart will always be with with my husband Han Kim. We have been together since high school and our daughter Yuri Kim who just is our angel, you be in good hands with her father. I'm holding back the tears but it hurts. My beloved siblings sister Shin, we were very close, and brother Chang, always playing around with me, who were always there for my support. Both of my parents died years ago, I hope to see them again soon. We live in Gan Gnam in South Korea a quiet neighborhood. First Lieutenant Joon Hyun (male), I leave behind my entire world, my beautiful wife Bora Hyun. We don't have any children but were planning to soon. Our love will remain forever, my brother Yang died years ago, I only hope to see him again. We live in the neighborhood Samcheong-Dong in South Korea, I will be with my parents and her from far away, protecting them always. Second Lieutenant Nam Sun (male), let me first say I so proud of my fellow soldiers who fought fiercely and endlessly until the very end. They came with overwhelming numbers and infantry ground forces. The blast caused an explosion that ended up quickly. I actually saw some fellow soldiers bleeding out because they were missing their limbs. Let me begin this next stage of the uncertainty of what's to come. I leave behind my fiancé Min Ji, we were going to marry right after this battle. She was everything to me, we were planning to have children, but this war has changed everything. My sister Jung Hyun, I only hope see will alright without me. My parents will keep her safe and visit me at the cemetery where I rest with my other family of soldiers. We live in the quiet neighborhood in Seoul N Tower in South Korea. I will forever miss all the moments and memories we have created, I will try my best to watch over them if I'm allowed to do so. Medical Staff Eunji Jung (female), no one was expecting this but here we are. I leave behind my husband Wook Jung, we have been together since school. Our two boys Jun Woo and A Jung, just as we were planning a family Reunion. This war has stopped everything, I will try to extend my love to them far away as much as possible. My siblings brother Hyeon, always cheering me on, my other brother Jeong, I was very close with my siblings and I miss them so much. We live in Myeong Dong in South Korea, my parents live close by also, everyone will be deeply missed. Warrant Officer Pae Chu (Male), I reserve my emotions but I'm shattered inside. I leave behind the love of my life my wife Do Yun. We were recently married and were planning to have a family. She is pregnant, we decided to be surprised on the gender. Let me continue as my eyes are in tears, everything happens for a reason. I will be with them always as time passes. My parents who have always been there, my sister Jin, who I admire so much, I know they will comfort my wife and the baby. We live in the city of Hongdae in South Korea. Medical Staff A Yeong Hun (female), as the tears come running down my face. I will compose myself and find my strength to tell my story. I leave behind beloved husband Jeong Hun, we have been together for such a long time. Our sweet boy Shin, I will miss them so much. My only hope is that he continues playing baseball and becomes a great player. My parents which are so close to me, both of my sisters Hyo Sonn and Mi-Cha, I couldn't ask for better siblings. We live so close together in a quiet neighborhood in the city of Apgujeong in South Korea. Sergeant Major Cho Seo (male), I didn't stop fighting, I never stopped, it was to much of them. Coming from everywhere, I was hit so many times by 120mm. It blew me up into pieces, I leave behind my darling wife Chohee Seo, the love of my life. My little girl Bom Seo, if only I can come back, I will try my best to comfort you sweetheart. My brother Choe, he also wants a career in the military, my parents that helped me out so much throughout life. We live in the city of Gwanghamun in South Korea, all our happy memories will stay in their hearts. Master Sergeant Yoo Jeon (male), let me see if I take a deep breath first to begin. I just want to say I didn't see it coming. The explosion was sudden and deadly, it took me out instantly. Let me say, I am so proud to die along with my fellow soldiers. I leave behind my love, Byeol Jeon, she was everything to me. Love, I will find a way to come back, my beautiful kids Bo Bae (daughter) and Yun (son). I would give anything to see them right now, the tears are pouring down my face. I only hope my parents can give Byeol the support and comfort she needs, I know they will, I am the only child. We all live together in the city of Insa-Dong in South Korea, so many happy times there. Sergeant First Class Chon Ryu (male), being on the battlefield is a description like no other. One part of you is actually there, the other is like in a dream from hell. Seeing dead bodies everywhere knowing that anything can happen. When it did it came with no mercy, the shelling was endless and we were out numbered badly. We finally died like brave soldiers, we take an oath and live by this to protect our country. I leave behind my gorgeous wife Seul Gi, she is so intelligent and sweet, our beloved children son Ji. Quite a baseball player I might add, I would always coach him and give him confidence. Let me gather my voice as I can't explain how much I will miss him. Our sweet daughter Da Eun, she is quite a gymnast, she is so gifted and my heart is crushed. My brother Beak and other brother Cho, they will both be crushed but everyone knows anything can happen in battle. If people knew the reality behind wars and destruction caused by war and the affects on the families and soldiers. We live in the quiet neighborhood in the city of Itaewon in South Korea. Medical Staff Chohee Kang (female), the minute we saw the infantry ground forces in overwhelming numbers. I knew we were in trouble, the missiles were being launched and the explosions were everywhere. It was instant, we died with honor and bravery giving medical assistance to our fellow soldiers. With that said, let me begin to tell you what I left behind. I'll compose myself, first it's my sweet husband Yang Kang. We have been planning to have a family, but not all plans go as planned. My beloved parents who has always been supportive of me. Both of my sisters Paenji and Dae, bless their hearts, both of them want to pursue a career in the medical field as I did. We live in the city of Namdaemun in South Korea. My love will be with them forever, I'll watch over them. Staff Sergeant Seok Chay (male), I was one of the first to die, we were in the blunt of the hell coming to us. I never stopped firing back, never, there was too many of them coming in every direction. Man, is this tough now, my tears are running down my face. I leave behind the sweetest wife ever Eun Hye Chay. The memories will leave behind will keep me warm, our two daughters, Daehyun and Donghyun. Talk about the sweetest girls ever. Both of our parents who live close by, My only brother Kim, I know his heart is hurting. I will try to watch over them as much as possible as they visit me at the cemetery, we all live in the city of Haebangchon in South Korea, so many memories I leave behind. Sergeant Yun Baek (male), look I'm not going to make any excuses I've been in battle my whole life. My nickname is bulldog, but this one was very intense and it caught us by surprise. They out numbered us by many foes, but we were the first to die, proudly and honorably. I leave behind my girlfriend and fiancé Eun Hee Baek, we were going to marry right after this this madness was more calm. We have no children but we were planning to, both of our parents who are amazing in every way. My three siblings brother Jang, sister Hyun Ae, sister Mun Hee, remember me as a brave soldier always, who made the ultimate sacrifice. We live in the city of Jamsil in South Korea, a nice quiet neighborhood. Corporal Ma Shin (male), we died instantly with the endless shelling and explosions. It ripped me in half, but we died as true soldiers. I'm very proud to die with my battalion to the very end. This war has been a total disaster, I leave behind my beloved wife Do Yoon Shin. I can't even begin to tell you how special she is in my heart. What hurts the most is our precious boy Si Woo, he loves soccer. I hope to see him excel into a great player, my parents who are my superhero's. My brother Choi, I know he is hurting, I wish I can take back what happened but this is reality now. We live in the city of Sinsa in South Korea, both me and my boy would train with the soccer ball in the park. Private First Class Ye Joon Gwan (male), to describe being inside of this hell, it takes so much pain and hatred from both sides. We stood our ground and were fighting back fiercely with no end. When suddenly a 120mm hit me directly on my shoulder. Tore my entire shoulder and arm off, I was bleeding out really bad. I saw the explosion of the missiles take out my fellow soldiers. I only stayed alive to witness this moment like it was meant to be. With my heart shattered into pieces I will begin to tell what I left behind. I want to first express we all died with honor and brave. My adorable wife that has been with me since school. She is my rock and support, Eun Hye Gwan, so bright and smart about everything. Our twin boys Wook and Siwoo, my tears are running down my face. What can I tell them now, I know my parents will try to support her with them. They are really smart and intelligent, they received that from their mother. My siblings brother Chong, sister Kwan and other sister Mun Hee, man, my heart is bleeding right now. We live in a quiet and peaceful neighborhood in the city of Daehangno in South Korea. Private Soojin Nam (male), we are the grunts, we are inside the line of fire and are always the first ones to die. There's no mercy in the battlefield, it's a fight for survival and brute courage. Going straight into hell is something that only an insane person does. With that said, I was killing so many of them, but just kept coming in larger numbers. Between the 120mm and shelling everywhere, straight hits on us. I saw myself ripped wide open, I only saw my fellow soldiers burning alive. I took it like a fearless soldier, died next to my family of soldiers. Let me begin to tell you my story, even though, it hurts so much. I leave behind my beautiful wife Jiu Nam, wow, what an amazing woman and recent mom. She is simply spectacular, we have two children, our daughter JunA and our son Yejoon. We were planning to have another child in the near future but this will never happen now. My beautiful parents that have always gave me the courage I have today. My brother Jon and other brother Jeon, this is harder than I thought, I will try to watch over all of them as much as I'm allowed. We live in a very unique neighborhood where everyone knows each other. Inside South Korea, let me add many of us were always constantly saying why in the hell our we killing our own people. On behalf, of the estimated 2.5 million lives lost after all the numbers were calculated including both sides in total. The bloodshed between our disagreements and political views. Want you have heard is only a fraction of the personal stories of the men and women that departed in this insane war. Each pouring their hearts out so the living can understand how war actually affects the soldiers in the front lines. Now, as a surprise to everyone, the so called enemy is right here with us and we don't hate each other. Now, the living can hear the North Korean soldiers tell their stories to what actually happened. Now, you will hear their personal stories and hopefully find answers to stop future wars from ever taking place.

Let's begin, June 25, 1950, under the command of Kim Il Sung, politician and founder of North Korea. KPA I Corps (53,000 men), drove across the Imjin river toward Seoul. The II Corps (54,000 soldiers), attacked along two widely separated axes. One through the cities of Ch' unch' on and Inje to Hongch' n and the other down the east coast road towards Kangnung. North Korean ground forces formations which fought in the Korean War included the I Corps, the II and III Corps, the IV Corps and V Corps, VI and VII Corps were formed after the outbreak of the war. August 15, 1948, was the greatest day for us when we saw with our own eyes the establishment of North Korea. Our great leader Kim Il Sung, indoctrinated our minds and spirits with looking at our brothers and sisters in South Korea as poison. A democracy that brings poison to our world, and we are superior with our ideologies. With that said, on June 25, 1950, we stormed into South Korea. The term we used was the liberation of Korea itself. Bring us together under a strong powerful Korea, as it once was under Japanese colonization. 100,000 troops proudly invaded Seoul. It was the proudest moment of our lives, we felt invincible. September 12, 1950, we advanced after months of fighting and controlled 5,000-square-mile rectangle centered on the critical southeastern port Pusan, also known as the Pusan Perimeter. Major events happened afterwards which created a hell of untold proportions. Afterwards, many major events happened, one of those happened on December 6, 1950. In the Chosin Reservoir, it was serious firepower on both sides. The dead bodies lay on the ground endlessly and many just pieces of them. If this isn't hell I don't know what is, our Corps fought fiercely. There was no going back, any soldiers that retreat will be executed on the spot. There is no cowards here, we constantly march forward. Many of our Corps were wiped out in this battle, to actually witness this will stay on your mind forever. Our Corp barely survived this battle, my heart bleeds in misery because we lost so many of our fellow soldiers. On January 4, 1951, we claim victory once again by recapturing Seoul. Now, we taste are strength once again. There's no to time to celebrate, this is way too early to claim victory over the Peninsula. For one moment we all felt good and proud. On April 25, 1951, all that will change, the Battle of Kapyong Imjin River. Is a day our Corp and many other Corps will never forget. My name is Senior Colonel Choh M-Yawng Naw. I am the leader of our proud men in my Corp. that day, it was holy hell that day. We stood our ground proudly, the infantry ground forces, missile systems, artillery systems, armored vehicles and everything else. Proved to much for many of our Corps, I really have to congratulate the other side from South Korea for their courage and bravery in this battle. Unfortunately, myself and my entire Corp were completely wiped out. Now, I join my fellow soldiers to give our testimonies one by one. So the world can see what it actually feels like to be in a hell like war from the other side. I am very humbled to be allowed to tell my story and my fellow soldiers in our Corp. this will only be a fraction of them, because the dead are endless.

As you know, my name is Senior Colonel Choh M-Yawng Naw (male), we were hit with everything, an explosion took me out instantly, I only saw my Corp die like proud and brave men. I leave behind my beautiful wife Ryom Tae Ok. She was my smile every day, our daughters Jung and Hei. Now, my only wish is for them to be the ballerinas they have always wanted. I will watch over them as much as I can, my mother who is still alive, because my father died not too long ago. I'm wishing to see him soon, my siblings sister Pak Chong Ae, and brother Jahng Sawng Tehk, I've always tried to prepare them for this moment but actually living it, its another story. We all in the province of Chagang in North Korea. I leave behind so many memories and moments. Colonel Lieutenant Yuhn Hyuhng (male) we serve proudly and our completely devoted to country and ideologies. It is embedded in our blood and in our souls. I congratulate the other side as they fought very bravely. I saw with my own eyes my men blown into pieces. I saw myself ripped limbs and bleeding out. We all died like the true soldiers we are, it is our honor. I leave behind my adorable wife Cha Hyo Sim, she is so talented and a wonderful wife. Our son Seo, who we were very close, and loved to play basketball. I will try my best to comfort them, my parents who saw me grow up from nothing to who I am today. My close brother Cheh Soo Hohn, he has always admired me as an older brother, now, I hope he can pull through this. We live in the province of North Hamgyong in North Korea. The memories I leave behind is a lot to bare. Colonel Major Moon Jawng Chuhl (male), I never would have thought that this would have been my day of battle. The others fought fiercely and nonstop. Even though, my men stood their ground, we were are hit with a barrage of artillery and shelling. My last sight was getting blown up along with my men. Now, I see myself on the other side, let me begin to tell you that since I enlisted myself and everyone else our indoctrinated hatred and more hatred towards our brothers and sisters from South Korea. I speak truth, I left behind my beautiful wife Choe Hyon Hwa, without a doubt my everything in life. We don't have any children because she can't but I still love her very much. We shared everything together and kept on trying to have a child but nothing. My parents that have always been true patriots of our cause and country. My sweet sisters Kim Yo Jong, and my other sister Choe Son Hui, they would tell me what are they supposed to do when I'm gone. We live in the province of South Hamgyong in North Korea, all the memories, all the love, I will try to comfort them. Captain Kihm Ihl Chuhl (male), it was ugly, war is ugly, we march forward and fight because retreating leads to an execution on site. I swear I didn't stop firing back, the shelling proved to be way too much from the other side. I saw my men torn into pieces by explosions and shelling. In the last moment I saw my leg on the ground and blood out instantly. Now, comes the hard part, I leave behind my wife of many years Yeonmi Park. She was an excellent wife and mom, loved to sow and make so many beautiful outfits and things. Our daughter Mee, quite a gymnast, very flexible and she loves it. I wonder how she will end up now without her father, I will watch over them as much as possible. My sweet parents. My two siblings sister Lee Ae Ran, she is exactly like our mom, and my brother Noh-Too-Churl, man, it hurts me so much to them all crying over me at the cemetery. We live in the province of North Hwang Hae in North Korea. Senior Lieutenant Lee Guhn (male), we will caught by surprise, just holy hell unfolded. The explosions were everywhere and it stuck us directly. All we saw was a noise and lights out, lucky bastards. Death was quick and without mercy, I prefer to go out this way. Give me a moment to compose my tears, I leave behind my sweet wife Kim Kuk Hyang. What an amazing woman and outstanding mom, we have two children. Yun our son, couldn't ask for a better kid. Our daughter Min, the most beautiful daughter. My tears our falling so much thinking I will never see them ever. I only hope both our parents can look after them, I know in my heart they will. My older sister Moon Ye Bong, she's been very close and supportive throughout my military service. We live in the province of Kangwon inside North Korea. First Lieutenant Lee Sawl Joo (male), I thought I've seen the worst by witnessing in a previous war a fellow soldier getting run over by a tank. This hell came out of nowhere, we were so confident with previous victories. This day the last thing I shall was my group of soldiers getting hit directly by the shelling and explosions. What I saw dying was my men's body parts everywhere. We all died like true soldiers, now, I find myself on the other side. Let me wipe my tears away, I leave behind my beloved wife Kim Hye Gyong. What am going to do now without her, we were so close. My mother, my father died a few years ago. Hopefully, I will see him again and be given permission to watch over our boy Ko. Quite a honor student and great son, I miss them so much. My brother Yahng Hyahng Sawp, he will surely miss me but I'm always close. We live in the province of North Pyongan inside North Korea. Second Lieutenant Kumgang Koom Gahng (male), I'm not going to sugar coat this. I feel so many emotions right now, the shelling was extraordinary from the other side. I knew we were in trouble when I saw one of our helicopters blow up right in front of us. Seeing that massive explosion with burning flesh everywhere was a sign from hell. Next, it was direct hits everywhere. I was hit many times, my arm and legs ripped off. It was an instant death, I saw the sky for the last time. Now, comes the hard part, what I leave behind is my entire world. My beautiful wife and partner Ko Kwang Hi, I can't express how special she is. Our beloved daughters Bitna and Ara, what in the hell am I supposed to do now. Why, did this war have to happen in the first place. Many of us kept saying why in the hell our we killing our own brothers and sisters in the same Peninsula. We know we cannot give our opinions without being executed on the spot. I'll try my best to watch over them as best as I could, my lovely parents our there to help out. Both of my brothers Hwahng Chahng Yawp, and Pahk Ghinhl Yohn, I'm sorry brothers but they understand I died for country and honor. We live in the province of South Pyongan inside North Korea. Now, enlisted troops, divided into NCO's and troopers. Sub dived into six ranks, Master Sergeant Yee Cheh

Suhn (male), the only way of describing this war is one hell after another. Being on the battlefield you already have a front row seat to death. It comes anywhere and at anytime, all one can do is fight endlessly. By the time we our engaged in battle our minds our full of so much hatred. We our soldiers and refusal is certain death. This day felt different, it was heavy firing from the opposition. In one instant I saw one of men head explode. The next minute a massive explosion that wiped us out. If there were anyone alive it was for a brief moment only. Now, I see myself here and I'll try to tell my story now. I leave behind my wife Hyon Song Wol, she was so sweet and talented. Many talents and gifts that resonated to our children. Our handsome boys Pak and Ju, who themselves came out so talented. One is a prospect in soccer with so many possibilities. The other is a gymnast, watching both of them made me so proud. What happens now, I know my parents will watch over them. My parents who I love so much, my beloved sister Ko Kwang Za, best sister ever, I know she is hurting right now. We live in the province of Ryanggang inside North Korea. Senior Sergeant Pahk Pawng Joo (male), let me try to explain how it feels to be in the front lines. It's like being in a living hell, seeing your fellow comrades in pieces with missing limbs on the ground. It is listening to the constant noises of roaring shelling and explosions everywhere. With that said, all my indoctrinated hatred since joining the military. It all came to an end on this day, the last I saw was a massive explosion that took out everyone. Myself, I was bleeding out from everywhere, death was instant. I guess this is being lucky, with next chapter is pretty tough. I leave behind my adorable wife Han Pil Hwa, she always knew that being a soldier's wife is extremely difficult. Knowing at anytime it's bye bye, I myself was always prepared for this. Our beautiful kids, this one hurts, our daughter little princess Chin. Man, what I'm going to do now, man, heart is shredded. Our amazing boy Lee, he is such a gifted son, and best friend. An excellent wrestler top in his school with scouts watching him. I hope he becomes something important, I will try my best to watch over them. My parents who are my angels, my closest sister Ri Sol Ju, amazing sister that gave me plenty of love, and my other sister Hana, she is a bit more distance because of her studies. We live in the province of North Hwanghae inside North Korea. Sergeant 1st Class Cheh Yawng Lihm (male), we had a front row seat into this hell. Watching an overwhelming artillery ground forces and missile systems come into this theater is unforgettable. I tired my best to hold back the opposition but they were relentless. In an instant I saw so many explosions and for a glimpse I saw my family. Now, this part is equally difficult leaving behind my true love my wife Kim Myung Sun. What a woman and excellent wife, one tough mom also. She keeps in line are two boys, who respect her and love her dearly. Han, is a perfect image of his mom, extremely smart and excels in his school work. Rim, is exactly like myself, he is as tough as they come. He loves the martial arts Taekwondo, he has so much potential. Both make me so proud, I know my mother will help her out with them. My father passed away a few years ago, I hope I see him soon. My beloved siblings brother Hyon, and other brother Ryang, we were so what close and played sports with each other. It was always intense games in any sport we played. We live in the province of Chagang inside North Korea. NCO's Sergeant Hahng Sawng Yawl (male), being in mud and right in the heart of the battle is my life. I've seen everything, my men blown up into pieces to bleeding out with no limbs. This battle was especially brutal, this day we were hit with so many artillery systems from different directions. When we saw the XK2 Black Panther tank firing its 120mm. I was hit immediately, torn off limbs and bleeding out seeing my men viciously fighting back until the explosion. We all died with honor and grace, I salute the other side, they got us. Now, here I am telling my story, what I left behind is my other family. First, is my lovely wife Pak So Hyang, sweet and beautiful, full of life. Now, I'm going to miss her very much, the tears are coming down. Our beautiful children, our son Sim, what a special young man. Very talented pianist, he is very dedicated and loves it. Our daughter Mishil, quite a ballerina, she trains so much. I will try my best to watch over them, I knew this day would come. Here there are no enemies, everyone is the same, we are all just the same with no differences. My parents I will miss very much, they will help out in my absence. My two sisters Chin Sun, and Gyeong Hui, they are both tough as they come, I know they will miss me a great deal. We live in the province of Kangwon inside North Korea. NCO's Corporal Cheh Jihn Soo (male), those bastards got lucky, it was hell and we were fighting hard and continuously. When suddenly all hell broke loose, between the missiles and seeing the K1A1 tank firing away at us. Direct hits, I actually saw one of my men split in half. He was still moving from the nervous system. The rest of us took direct hits as well, but at the end of the day we died with honor and bravery. Now, this part sucks, I leave behind my fiancé Ri Mi Gyong. We were going to get married soon and have a memorial wedding but now everything is uncertain. Our beautiful girl Eun Ju, the sweetest girl on earth. Such a bright student, she will definitely be hurt by my absence. Now, I only hope to be able to watch over them. I'm hoping to see my parents again which they died years ago. It was almost in the same year, they were truly in love with each other. I'm the only child so no one else has to suffer endlessly. We live in the province of Ryanggang inside North Korea. NCO's Private Trooper Ihm Tawng Ohk (male), being on front lines is a death sentence. Crawling through the mud and seeing death everywhere. I've seen everything, from my fellow soldiers being blown up by a live grenade to artillery fire. Either way, one must have the guts and courage to die with honor. This awful day, everything was miserable, taking nonstop fire. Those bastards got lucky, I was blown up into pieces along side my fellow soldiers. I've encountered so much in my life, but seeing myself on the other side. Everything here is completely different, no one is an enemy here. Let me wipe away my tears and begin to tell you what I leave behind. My sweet wife Ho Jong Suk, I cannot begin to tell you how many times she would wonder if I'm ever coming home from a battle. She was my rock and support emotionally and spiritually. Our beautiful children, daughter Dam Bi, the happiest girl on earth. She is so smart and has her mom's character. Excellent student, so talented in art and culture. Our sweet boy Shin, exactly like me. So gifted with sports, loves all the sports actually. How on earth am I going to protect them and watch over them now. My parents will definitely fill in the void, to help out as much as possible. My sweet sister Ha Neul, which is an amazing friend and sibling throughout my career. We live in the province of South Pyongan inside North Korea. I would do anything to return to those endless memories. NCO's Private Trooper Moon Ihl Bawng (male), facing death in every battle isn't easy. Hearing the explosions everywhere, constant shelling, machine gun fire. This is our world, the world of a soldier. On this particular day it was gruesome, we were pinned down in a roaring battle. When suddenly the explosions took us out, the last thing I saw was my men on fire. I myself was on fire also, the pain was overwhelming but I died swiftly. Now, let me begin to tell you what I leave behind. My wife of many years Jon Kyong Hui, my heart is crushed. What will she do now. I know her parents and siblings will comfort her. My brother Chae, and my amazing parents that always were there for me in good and bad times. Our daughter Sang, she is the sweetest girl ever. My tears are endless now, but I will try my best to watch over them. We live in the province of North Hamgyong inside North Korea. So many moments and now everything is uncertain, but we all died bravely and for our country. NCO's Private Trooper Kahng Chohl Hwahn (male), I'm not going to beat around the bush, it is stepping into hell. Both sides trying their best to kill one another. Our hatred comes from the very beginning of being enlisted to making ranks. This day was our unlucky day, no excuses, no regrets. I knew we were in trouble as the shelling became closer and closer. Describing death is like unbelievable pain and lights out. I only thing moments before were seeing my fellow soldiers screaming in pain without limbs and burnt everywhere. Now, this part is very strange because here we have no enemies. It makes you wonder why in hell did we even have this crazy war in the first place. I leave behind my wife since school Jong Kum Hwa, best thing that ever happened to me. We are always prepared for this, as a soldier's wife it is extremely difficult. My dear sister Yoona, and brother Byeon, especially my parents. We have two children, our two boys Jin, who excels in music, quite a talented musician I might add. Our other son Kwon, very talented in marshal arts and school work. Both are excellent boys and I'm so proud of them. I am very proud of them, I will find a way to watch over them. We live in the province of South Hamgyong inside North Korea.

I have returned, Lieutenant Colonel Lee Hong, from South Korea leader of the battalion. You have heard only a fraction of the heartbreaking testimonies from the men and women who were medical assistance. You have heard only a small fraction of the heartbreaking testimonies from the soldiers of North Korea. The testimonies are endless, with plenty of suffering and real life experiences on how it feels to actually be on the battlefield. Imagine, hearing all the testimonies from the men and women who sacrificed everything. If your heart isn't broken into pieces by now, let us salute all the brave and honorable men and women who died with courage and valor. Let us honor them for the rest of our lives, we never forget and we'll always remember. Let us always remember that everyone suffers in war, from the injuries, wounded, and especially the families that will keep their love burning into their souls forever. Our hearts also go out to the civilians on the peninsula of Korea, that faced this hell together. Let's begin, around 60,000 members of the British Armed Forces served in Korea, many were National Serviceman. British Forces: over 1,100 killed and 2,600 wounded. American Forces: nearly 37,000 killed and 92,000 wounded. South Korean Forces: at least half a million killed or wounded. Chinese Forces: over 110,000 killed and 380,000 wounded. North Korean Forces: at least half a million killed or wounded. Estimates suggest that at least two million North and South Korean civilians died. Let's proceed forward with the statistics and analysis of the Korean War. 1,789,000 Americans served in the war, with 36,574 deaths (battle deaths 33,739 other deaths 2,835), 103,284 wounded in action. As of 2014, prisoner of war POW's and missing in action MIA's is 8,176, total captured 7,245, killed in POW camps 2,806, returned 4,418, defectors 21, unaccounted 931. As of 2023, missing in action MIA's and unaccounted remains is 7,428. Casualty figures remain disputed but western estimates figure 400,000 Chinese deaths, while Chinese sources give a death toll of about 180,000 from the conflict. Total civilian deaths: 2-3 million estimated, South Koreans 990,968 casualties, North Koreans 1,550,000 casualties estimated. This is an overview of the countries that participated in the Korean War. In all, 21 countries from around the world came to fight for and help Korea during the Korean War.

These 16 countries sent fighting units to Korea (listed from largest to smallest military force). 1) USA, 2) Great Britain, 3) Canada, 4) Turkey, 5) Australia, 6) Philippines, 7) Thailand, 8) The Netherlands, 9) Colombia, 10) Greece, 11) New Zealand, 12) Ethiopia, 13) Belgium, 14) France, 15) South Africa. 16) Luxembourg. Medical units and aid were sent from these 5 countries, 17) Sweden, 18) Denmark, 19) India, 20) Norway, 21) Italy. After seeing so much death and destruction we will never forget their sacrifices. I myself have joined them and I am honored to be among such brave and honorable men and women. Let us now salute the women in this conflict, starting with the beloved partners and mothers across our world that have chosen to become part of the military family both in civilian and military service.

Let's begin, South Korea, conscription has existed since 1957 and requires male citizens between the ages of 18 and 35 to perform compulsory military service. Women are not required to perform military service, but they may voluntarily join the military. North Korea, emphasized the role of mothers and recognized the role of the housewife as a valid alternative to state employment. The country began this acknowledgment of housewives and mothers near its founding, with the 1946 Labour Law prohibiting women and children from "toilsom or harmful labour". In 2015, North Korea made military service mandatory for women between the ages of 17 and 20, women are required to serve until the age of 23. Women were still not drafted for Korea or Vietnam, though some 120,000 of them served on active duty during the Korean War, according to the Korean War Legacy Foundation. A third of those were in health care positions, including frontline mobile army surgical hospitals. In North Korea, women experience extreme oppression from men who are in positions of official authority. North Korea went through some horrific treatment and conditions. Women face in the military include sexual assault, brutal physical punishments, forced abortions, lack of feminine hygiene products, the use of threats to shame and silent women. Conscription in North Korea occurs despite ambiguity concerning legal status. Men are universally conscripted while women undergo selective conscription, conscription takes place at age 17 and service ends at 30. Our journey and destiny were written in blood and what we all witnessed on July 27, 1953. On a clear day with the shadows of our souls watching this historical moment.

Let's begin, the U.N. North Korea and China sign an armistice agreement, South Korea refuses to sign. The agreement calls for a 2.5-mile-wide-buffer zone across the middle of the Korean Peninsula that closely follows the 38th Parallel. A demilitarized zone (DMZ) was created by pulling back the respective forces 1.2 miles (2km) along each side of the boundary. It runs for about 150 miles (240km) across the peninsula, from the mouth of the Han River on the west coast to a little south of the North Korean town of Kosong on the best east coast. Located within the DMZ is the "Truce Village" of P'anmunjom, about 5 miles (8km) east of Koesong. It was the site of peace discussions during the Korean War and since been the location of various conferences over issues related to North and South Korea, their allies, and the UN. Even after this historical day that we all sacrificed so much and shed our blood and guts to make this happen. The hatred continued, the living never learn how to settle their differences. The endless incidents that occurred on the peninsula around the (DMZ) demilitarized zone. Let's recall the incidents one by one to get a better understanding on how hatred manifests.

Many of the incidents occurring at sea are due to border disputes. In 1977, North Korea claimed an Exclusive Economic Zone over a large area south of the disputed western maritime border, the northern limit line in the Yellow Sea. This is a prime fishing area, particularly for crabs, and clashes commonly occur, which have been dubbed the "crab war", as of January 2011, North Korea had violated the armistice 221 times, including 26 military attacks. There were also incursions into North Korea, in 1976, in now-declassified meeting minutes, U.S. Deputy Secretary of Defense William Clements told Henry Kissinger that there had been 200 raids or incursions into North Korea from the south, though not by the U.S. military. Details of only few of these incursions have become public, including raids by South Korean Forces in 1967 that had sabotaged about 50 North Korean facilities.

February 16, 1958: North Korean agents hijack a Korean Air Lines flight changlang en route from Busan to Seoul and land it in Pyongyang; one American pilot, two West German passengers, and 24 other passengers were released in early March, but eight other passengers remained in North Korea.

March 6, 1958: an American F-86 Sabre is shot down near the DMZ. The pilot (Leon Pfeiffer) was captured and released after 11 days.

May 17, 1963: an American OH-23 helicopter was shot down near the Korean DMZ. The crew (US Army Captains Ben W. Stutts and Carleton W. Voltz) were captured. They were released a year later on

May 16, 1964. 1964: North Korea creates an underground group: Revolutionary Party for Reunification, this group is ground down and eliminated by South Korean authorities by 1969.

September 27, 1964: four South Korean agents crossed the DMZ and killed 13 North Korean soldiers.

October 14, 1964: South Korea attempts an assassination of a Korean People's Army Division Commander.

April 27, 1965: two North Korean Mig-17s attack a United States Air Force RB-47 Sratojet reconnaissance plane above the Sea of Japan, 80km (50mi) from the North Korean shore. The aircraft was damaged, but managed to land at Yokota Air Base, Japan.

October 1966-1969: the Korean DMZ Conflict, a series of skirmishes along the DMZ, results in 75 American, 299 South Korean and 397 North Korean soldiers killed.

January 19, 1967: ROKS Dangpo (PCEC 56) (formerly the USS Marfa (PCE-8421), is sunk by North Korean coastal artillery north of the maritime demarcation line off the east coast of Korea, 39 sailors of the crew of 79 are killed.

October 18, 1968: in an incident known as the Blue House Raid, a 31-man detachment from Korean People's Army secretly crosses the DMZ on a mission to kill South Korean President Park Chung-Hee on January 21, nearly succeeding. The incursion was discovered after South Korean civilians confronted the North Koreans and informed the authorities. After entering Seoul disguised as South Korean soldiers, the North Koreans attempt to enter the Blue House (the official residence of the President of South Korea). The North Koreans were confronted by South Korean police and a firefight ensued. The

North Koreans fled Seoul and individually attempted to cross the DMZ back to North Korea, of the original group of 31 North Koreans, 28 were killed, one was captured, and two are unaccounted for. Additionally, 26 South Koreans were killed and 66 were wounded, the majority of whom were soldiers and police officers. Three American soldiers were also killed and three were wounded.

January 23, 1968: the U.S. Navy intelligence ship USS Pueblo was attacked by the Korean People's Navy employing soviet-built patrol boats and is substantially boarded and captured, along with its crew, in the Sea of Japan. The entire of 83 is captured, with the exception of one sailor killed in the initial attack on the vessel, and the vessel was taken to a North Korean port. Tortured during imprisonment, all the captures were released on December 23 of the same year via the bridge of no return at the DMZ. The USS Pueblo is still in North Korean possession and docked in Pyongyang on display as a museum ship. From March 1968 and March 1969, various military skirmishes took place in the Paektusan region between the North Korean and Chinese Armed Forces.

October 30, 1968: from October 30 to November 2, 120 to 130 North Korean unit 124 commandos land on the northeast shore of South Korea, allegedly to establish a base in order to wage a guerrilla war against the South Korean government. 70,000 ROK soldiers were involved in the ensuing search-and-destroy operation. A total of 110 to 113 North Korean commandos were killed. Seven were captured, and 13 escaped. A total of 40 South Korean soldiers and law enforcement officers were killed as well as 23 civilians.

March 1969: six North Korean commandos kill a South Korean police officer near Jumunjin, Gangwon-Do. Seven American soldiers are killed in a North Korean attack along the DMZ.

April 15, 1969: a U.S. Navy EC-121M warning star reconnaissance aircraft is shot down 90 miles (140km) in international waters east of the North Korean coast, leaving 31 dead,

August 17, 1969: three US soldiers were wounded and captured when their helicopter was shot down for straying into North Korean airspace. They were released 108 days later when the US apologized.

October 1969: four U.S. soldiers are killed by North Koreans in the DMZ. The four U.S. soldiers from the 7th infantry division were traveling in a truck marked with a white flag and labeled with a sign that said "DMZ POLICE" when they were ambushed by a North Korean patrol with rifle fire and grenades. The Koreans then went up to the to the truck and shot each soldier in the head at close range to ensure they were dead. The ambush killed Staff Sergeant James R. Grissinger, Specialist Charles E. Taylor, Specialist Jack L. Morris and Private First Class William E. Grimes.

December 11, 1969: North Korean agent Cho Chang-Hui hijacked a Korean Air Lines YS-11 flying from Gangneung Airbase in Gangneung, Gangwon-Do to Gimpo International Airport in Seoul. It was carrying four crew members and 46 passengers (excluding Cho); 39 of the passengers were returned two months later. But the crew and seven passengers remained in North Korea. The aircraft was damaged beyond repair on landing.

April 1970: at Kumchon, Gyeon GGI-DO a crash leaves three North Korean infiltrators dead and five South Korean soldiers wounded.

June 1970: the Korean People's Navy seizes a broadcast vessel from the South near the Northern Limit Line. 20 crew are captured.

February 1974: two South Korean fishing vessels are sunk and 30 crew detained by the North.

June 1974: three North Korean gunboats attacked and sank a Korea Coast Guard Patrol Craft (863) in the Sea of Japan near the maritime demarcation border. 26 South Korean Guardmen killed. South Korean and North Korean fighter jets engage each other over the sea battle but do not fire upon each other.

1974: the first North Infiltration Tunnel into South Korea is discovered. Three following tunnels were found in 1975, 1978, 1990. The joint South Korean-U.S. investigation team trip a Korean Booby-Trap, killing one American and wounding six others.

March 1975: the second North Korean infiltration tunnel is discovered.

June 1976: an incursion south of the DMZ in Gangwon-Do leaves three dead from the the North and six from the South.

August 18, 1976: the axe murder incident-attempt to trim a tree in the DMZ near P'anmun-jom-ends with two U.S. soldiers dead and injuries to another for U.S. soldiers and five South Korean soldiers.

July 14, 1977: a U.S. Army CH-47 Chinook helicopter is shot down after straying into the North over the DMZ.

Three airmen are killed and one is briefly held prisoner (this was the sixth such incident since the armistice was signed). The Carter Administration apologized for the incident and paid reparations to North Korea.

October 1978: the third North Korean infiltration tunnel is discovered.

October 27, 1979: U.S. patrol fired at night after the assassination of South Korean President Park.

October 28, 1979: three North Korean agents attempting to infiltrate the eastern sector of the DMZ are intercepted, killing one of the agents.

December 6, 1979: a U.S. patrol in the DMZ accidentally crosses the MDL into North Korean minefield in heavy fog. One U.S. soldier is killed and four are injured; the body is recovered from North Korea five days later.

March 1980: three North Koreans are killed while trying to cross the Han River Estuary into the South.

May 1980: North Koreans engage USIROK OUTPOST OUILLETTE on the DMZ in a firefight. One North Korean is wounded in action.

March 1981: three North Koreans try to enter South Korea in Geumhwa-Eup, Cheorwon, Gangwon-Do; one is killed.

July 1981: three North Koreans are killed trying to cross the upper Imjin River to the South.

May 1982: two North Korean infiltrators are spotted on the east coast, with one being killed.

December 1983: U.S. soldiers encounter attempted infiltration of North Korean soldiers over the MDL south into but American sector but were repelled by the QRF deployed from camp Greaves, South Korea.

April 1984: South Korean agents the DMZ near the Imjin River, a single agent killed by a landmine with body recovered by North Korean soldiers.

November 23, 1984: three North Korean soldiers and one American soldier wounded in a firefight that broke out after a Soviet defector fled across the DMZ into South Korea.

November 1987: one American soldier and two North Korean soldiers die, and one American soldier is wounded during the firefight that erupted when a North Korean security detail confronted a sniper detail across the MDL into the southern-controlled sector of the Joint Security Area.

November 1987: one South Korean killed at the DMZ central sector by North Korean sniper fire.

March 1990: the fourth North Korean infiltration tunnel is discovered, in what may be a total of seventeen tunnels in all.

May 1992: three North Korean in South Korean uniforms are killed at Cheorwon, Gangwon-Do; three South Korean soldiers are wounded.

December 17, 1994: a U.S. Army OH-584+ Kiowa helicopter inadvertently crosses 10 km into North Korean territory and is shot down. Of the crew of two, one dies and the other is held for 13 days. The Clinton Administration apologized for the incident and paid reparations to North Korea.

May 1995: North Korean forces fire on a South Korean fire on a South Korean fishing boat, killing three.

October 1995: two armed North Koreans are discovered at the Imjin River; one is killed.

April 1996: several hundred armed North Korean troops enter the DMZ at the Joint Security Area and elsewhere on three occasions, in violation of the Korean Armistice Agreement.

May 1996: seven northern soldiers cross the DMZ, but withdraw after warning shots are fired.

May & June 1996: North Korean vessels twice cross the Northern Limit Line and have a several hour standoff with the South Korean navy.

September 1996: a North Korean Sang-O-class submarine inserts a reconnaissance team and runs aground on the east coast of South Korea near Jeongdongjin, 20 kilometres south-east of Gangneung. Gangwon-Do, leading to a 49-day manhunt for the 25 crewmen.

April 1997: five North Korean soldiers cross the DMZ in Chelwon, Gangwon-Do and fire on South Korean positions.

June 1997: three North Korean vessels cross the Northern Limit Line and attack South Korean vessels two miles (3km) south of the line. On land, fourteen North Korean soldiers cross 70 m south of the center of the DMZ, leading to a 23-minute exchange of fire.

June 1998: a North Korean Yugo-class submarine became entangled in a fishing drifnet, it was salvaged on 25 June and the bodies of nine crewmen were recovered all dead by gunshot wounds.

July 1998: a dead North Korean frogman was found with paraphernalia on a beach south of the DMZ.

June 1999: the First Battle of Yeonpyeong, a series of clashes between North and South Korea vessels, takes place in the Yellow Sea near the Northern Limit Line.

October 26, 2000: two U.S. aircraft observing a ROK army military exercise accidentally cross the DMZ. The Clinton Administration apologized for the incident and paid reparations to North Korea.

2001: on twelve separate occasions, North Korean vessels cross the Northern Limit Line and then withdraw.

November 27, 2001: North and South Korean forces exchange fire without injuries.

June 29, 2002: the second battle of Yeonpyeong leads to the deaths of six South Korean sailors and the sinking of a South Korean vessel. The number of North Koreans killed is unknown.

November 16, 2002: South Korean forces fire warning shots on a Northern boat crossing the Northern Limit Line, the boat withdraws. The similar incident is repeated on November 20.

February 19, 2003: a North Korean fighter plane crosses seven miles (11km) south of the Northern Limit Line, and returns north after being intercepted by six South Korean planes.

March 2, 2003: four North Korean fighter jets (two MIG-29's and possibly two MIG-135S cobra ball reconnaissance plane over the Sea of Japan. US officials later alleged that they intended to force the plane to land in North Korea and take the crew as hostages.

July 17, 2003: North and South Korean forces exchange fire at the DMZ around 6am. The South Korean army reports four rounds fired from the North and seventeen from the South. No injuries are reported.

November 1, 2004, North Korean vessels, claiming to be in pursuit of illegal fishing craft, cross the Northern Limit Line and are fired upon by the South, the vessels withdraw 3 hours later.

May 26, 2006: two North Korean soldiers enter the DMZ and into South Korea. They return after South Korean soldiers fire warning shots.

July 30, 2006: several gunshots are exchanged near a South Korean post in Yanggu, Gangwon.

October 27, 2009: a South Korean pig farmer, who was wanted for assault, cut a hole in the DMZ fence and defected to North Korea.

November 10, 2009: naval vessels from the two Koreas exchanged fire In the area of the NLL, reportedly causing serious damage to a North Korean patrol ship. For more details of this incident, see Battle of Daecheong.

January 27, 2010: North Korea fires artillery shells into the water near Baengnyeong Island and South Korean vessels return fire. Three days later, North Korea continued to fire artillery towards the area.

March 26, 2010: A Republic of Korea Navy vessel, the ROKS Cheonan, was allegedly sunk by a North Korean torpedo near Baenyeong Island in the Yellow Sea. A rescue operation recovered 58 survivors but 46 sailors were killed. On

May 20, 2010: a South Korean led international investigation group concluded that the sinking of the warship was in fact the result of a North Korea torpedo attack. North Korea denied involvement. The United Nations Security Council made a Presidential Statement condemning the attack but without identifying the attacker.

October 29, 2010: two shots are fired from North Korean post near Hwacheon and South Korean troops fire three shots in return.

November 23, 2010: North Korea fired artillery at South Korea's Greater Yeonpyeong Island in the Yellow Sea and the Republic of Korea Armed Forces returned fire. Two South Korean marines and two South Korean civilians were killed. Six were seriously wounded, and ten were treated for minor injuries. About seventy South Korean houses were destroyed. North Korean casualties were unknown, but Lee Hong-Gi, the Director of Operations of the South Korean Joint Chiefs of Staff (JCS), claimed that as a result of the South Korean retaliation "there may be a considerable number of North Korean casualties".

October 6, 2012: an 18-year-old Korean People's Army Private defected to South Korea. He was apparently not detected as he crossed the DMZ and had to knock on an ROK barracks door to draw attention to himself. The soldier later told investigators that he defected after killing two of his superiors.

September 16, 2013: Nam Yong-Ho, a 47-year-old South Korean, was shot dead by South Korean soldiers while trying to swim across the Tanpocheon Stream near Paju to North Korea. He had previously made an application for political asylum in Japan, but this was rejected.

February 26, 2014: South Korean defense officials claim that despite warnings a North Korean warship has repeatedly crossed into South Korean waters overnight.

March 24, 2014: A North Korean drone is found crashed near Paju. The in onboard cameras contain pictures of the Blue House and military installations near the DMZ. Another North Korean drone crashes on Baengnyeongdo on March 31.

October 10, 2014: North Korean forces fire anti-aircraft rounds at propaganda balloons launched from Paju. South Korean military return fire after a warning.

October 19, 2014: A group of North Korean soldiers approach the South Korean border and South Korean soldiers fire warning shots. The North Korean soldiers return fire before retreating. No injuries or property damage results.

June 15, 2015: A teenaged North Korean soldier walks across the DMZ and defects at a South Korean guard post in north-eastern Hwacheon.

August 4, 2015: two South Korean soldiers were wounded after stepping on landmines that had allegedly been laid on the southern side of the DMZ by North Korean forces next to a ROK guard post. Kim Jin-Moon of the South Korean-based Korea Institute for Defense Analyses. Suggested that the incident was planned by members of the General Bureau of Reconnaissance to prove their loyalty to Kim Jong Un.

August 20, 2015: As a reaction to the August 4 landmines, South Korea resumed playing propaganda on loudspeakers near the border. In 2004 both sides had agreed to end their loudspeaker broadcasts at each other. North Korea threatened to attack those loudspeakers, and on August 20 North Korea fired a rocket and shells across the border into Yeoncheon County. South Korea responded by firing artillery shells back at the origin of the rocket. There were no reports of injuries on either side. Following threats of war from the North, and various troop movements by both North and South Korea and the University

States, an agreement was reached on August 24 that North Korea wound express sympathy for the landmine incident in return for South Korea deactivating the loudspeakers.

January 3, 2016: South Korean soldiers fired warning shots at a suspected North Korean drone near the DMZ.

November 13, 2017: North Korean soldier Oh Chong-Song defected by crossing the demarcation line in the JSA. The defector was shot by other KPA soldiers and was found about 55 yards (165ft; 50m) from the demarcation line.

November 15, 2017: An American citizen was arrested by South Korean forces for crossing the civilian control line just outside the DMZ as part of an attempt to get into North Korea"for political purposes", authorities said.

December 21, 2017: A North Korean soldier crossed the DMZ to defect to South Korea 40 minutes later shots were fired on the North Korean side of the DMZ, though the defectors was not fired upon.

August 12, 2018: A South Korean citizen was arrested for attempting to illegally enter North Korea. According to the reports, a 34-year-old man surnamed Suh drove an SUV through the checkpoint on the Unification Bridge in Paju, Gyeonggi province, which leads to the Demilitarized Zone separating the two Koreas. Without undergoing proper inspection. Suh was caught by South Korean troops at the joint security area of P'anmunjom, at a reservoir located 6 kilometers (3.7mi) away from the bridge. This was Suh's second known attempt to enter North Korea.

November 16, 2018: A South Korean soldier died after being found with a gunshot wound to his head at a toilet within a guard post (GP) on the eastern section of the border with North Korea. The death was ruled to be a suicide.

May 3, 2020: A South Korean guard post inside the DMZ was hit by multiple bullets coming from North Korea, prompting South Korea to broadcast a warning and return fire twice. Afterwards, South Korea took action via the Inter-Korean communication channels to prevent further incidents.

September 22, 2020: A South Korean official (Lee Dae-Jin) of The Ministry of Maritime Affairs and Fisheries disappeared from his patrol boat that was 6 miles (5.2 nmi; 9.7km) south of the NLL. He was found wearing a life jacket by a North Korean fishing patrol, which was ordered to shoot him and burn his body. North Korea's leader Kim Jong Un apologized to South Korea's leader Moon Jae-In for killing the South Korean official.

December 26, 2022: five North Korean drones cross the DMZ into South Korea, which scrambled aircraft to intercept them, one of the South Korean KA-1 light attack aircraft crashed during takeoff. It is believed that North Korea launched the drones in response to criticism of the quality of North Korean satellite images.

July 18, 2023: Travis King, a U.S. soldier who was at the border as part of a tour of the Joint Security Area, crossed the military demarcation line into North Korea and was detained by the North Korean military until his release on September 27.

Provocatory missile activities thus far in 2022, we have seen 22 North Korean ballistic missile launch events involving the launch of of 41 ballistic missiles-the most ballistic missile launch events and launches detected in any year to date, and it's only October. These include: thirty-one launches of solid-propellant short-range ballistic missiles (SRBMs), probably including the previously-tested KN-23, KN-24, and KN-25, as well as a new-type, smaller missile linked by the North Korean's to "tactical nukes". Two launches of a new maneuvering reentry vehicle (MaRV) on a liquid-propellant medium-range ballistic missile (MRBM) booster first tested in 2021: the North touted this as a second type of "hypersonic missile" that it claims has completed development. Two tests (one probable) of the Hwasong-12 liquid-propellant IRBM the first since 2017, with the North now claiming that series production and deployment of the system is either imminent or underway and a probable full-range (4,600km) test in October. Most significantly, the resumption of ICBM testing after more than four years (one successful), and up to four apparent scaled-down component tests (three successful), for the new, very large Hwasong-17 liquid-propellant missile. In addition, North Korea showcased a new, solid-propellant submarine-launched ballistic missile (SLBM) even larger than the Pukguksong-5 missile in its 2021 military parades, which also has not yet been flight tested. I have returned again, Lieutenant Colonel Lee Hong from the South Korean battalion. After hearing about how close we came after many incidents throughout another outbreak of war. One must think after so many of us died in battle and the overwhelming suffering to everyone around us. Especially, those who suffered extensive injuries and must continue their lives. Not to mention, the families of so many that must carry on but never forget. Let us now examine what exactly happened prior to the invasion from North Korea. We will also examine the history of Korea as a peninsula and most important, the periods in history when the peninsula was unified. It shall be examined closely the unification of the peninsula for good or bad perspectives and ideologies.

We shall start with the most current events and gradually go deep into the past to see and compare possibly how all this chaos originated from. Exactly where the hatred began and developed throughout our history in our Korean Peninsula. The Korean War had its immediate origins in the collapse of the Japanese empire at the end of World War II in September 1945, unlike China, Manchuria, and the former Western colonies seized by Japan in 1941-42, Korea, annexed to Japan since 1910, did not have a native government or a colonial regime waiting to return after hostilities ceased. Most claimants to power were harried exiles in China, Manchuria, Japan, the U.S.S.R., and the United States. They fell into two broad categories. The first was made up of committed Marxist revolutionaries who had fought the Japanese as part of the Chinese-dominated guerrilla armies in Manchuria and China. One of these exiles was a minor but successful guerrilla leader named Kim II-Sung, who had received some training in Russia and had been made a major in the Soviet army. The other Korean nationalist movement, no less revolutionary, drew its inspiration from the best of science, education, and industrialism in Europe, Japan, and America. These "ultranationalist" were split into rival factions, one of which centered on Syngman Rhee, educated in the United States and at one time the president of a dissident Korean Provisional Government in exile.

In their hurried effort to disarm the Japanese army and repatriate the Japanese population (estimated at 700,000), the United States and the Soviet Union agreed in August 1945 to divide the country for administrative purposes at the 38th parallel (latitude 38•n). At least from the American perspective, this geographic division was a temporary expedient; however, the Soviets began a short-lived reign of terror in northern Korea that quickly politicized the division by driving thousands of refugees south. The two sides could not agree on a formula that would produce a unified Korea, and in 1947 President Harry S. Truman persuaded the United Nations (UN) to assume responsibility for the country. Though the U.S. military remained nominally in control of the South until 1948. Both the South Korean national police and the constabulary doubled in size, providing a southern security force of about 80,000 by 1947. In the meantime, Kim II-Sung strengthened his control over the Communist Party as well as the northern administrative structure and military forces. In 1948 the North Korean military forces and police numbered about 100,000, reinforced by a group of southern Korean guerrillas based at Haeju in western Korea. The creation of an independent South Korea became UN policy in early 1948. Southern communists opposed this, and by autumn partisan warfare had engulfed parts of every Korean province below the 38th parallel. The fighting expanded into a limited border war between the south's newly formed Republic of Korea Army. (ROKA) and the North Korean border constabulary as well as the North Korean People's Army (KPA), the North launched 10 cross border guerrilla incursions in order to draw ROKA units away from their guerrilla-suppression campaign in the South. In its larger purpose the

Republic of Korea (ROK) was formed in August 1948, with Syngman Rhee as president. Nevertheless, almost 8,000 members of South Korean security forces and at least 30,000 other Koreans lost their lives. Many of the victims were not security forces or armed guerrillas at all but simple people identified as "rightists" or "reds" by the belligerents. Small-scale atrocious became a way of life. The partisan war also delayed the training of the South Korean army. In early 1950, American advisors judged that fewer than half of the ROKA's infantry battalions were even marginally ready for war. U.S. military assistance consisted largely of surplus. Indeed, General Douglas MacArthur, commander of the United States' Far East Command (FECOM), argued that his Eighth Army, consisting of four weak divisions in Japan, required more support than the Koreans. In early 1949 Kim Il-Sung pressed his case with Soviet leader Joseph Stalin that the time had come for a conventional invasion of the South. Stalin refused, concerned about the relative unpreparedness of the North Korean armed forces and about possible U.S. involvement. In the course of the next year, the communist leadership built the KPA into a formidable offensive force modeled after a Soviet mechanism army. The Chinese released Korean veterans from the People's Liberation Army, while the Soviets provided armaments. By 1950 the North Koreans enjoyed substantial advantages over the South in every category of equipment. After another Kim visit to Moscow in March-April 1950, Stalin approved an invasion. The National Liberation Day of Korea is a public holiday celebrated annually on 15 August in both South and North Korea. It commemorates the day when Korea was liberated from 35 years of Japanese colonial rule. The day marks the annual anniversary of the announcement the Japan would unconditionally surrender on August 15, 1945. All forces of the Imperial Japanese Army were ordered to surrender to the allies. Independent Korean governments were created three years later, on 15 August 1948. Korea has been an independent nation for centuries, but it had been invaded multiple times, with the last invasion being the period of Japanese rule. It took three years after korea became independent in 1945 for the nation to actually establish the Republic of Korea on August 15, when National Liberation Day, is celebrated. August 15th is celebrated by many countries as Victory Over Japan Day, the day Japan's Emperor announced the country's surrender. The United States, however, commemorators this day in September when the Japanese formally signed a declaration of surrender. Liberation Day is celebrated by both North Korea and South Korea. Japan first took Korea into its sphere of influence during the late 1800's. Both Korea (Joseon) and Japan had been under policies of isolationism, with Joseon being a tributary state of Qing China. However, in 1854, Japan was forcefully opened by the United States in the Perry Expedition. It then rapidly modernized under the Meiji Restoration, while Joseon continued to resist foreign attempts to open it up. Japan eventually succeeded in opening Joseon with the unequal Japan-Korea treaty of 1876. Afterwards, it embarked on a decades-long process of defeating its local rivals, securing alliances with Western powers, and asserting its influence in Korea. Japan assassinated the defiant Korean queen and intervened in the Donghak Peasant Revolution.

After Japan defeated China in the 1894-1895 First Sino-Japanese War, Joseon became nominally independent and declared the short-lived Korean Empire. Japan then defeated Russia in the 1904-1905 Russo-Japanese War, making it the sole regional power, it then moved quickly to fully absorb Korea. It first made korea a protectorate with the the Japan-Korea Treaty of 1905, and then ruled the country indirectly through the Japanese Resident-General of Korea. After forcing the Korean Gojong to abdicate in 1907, Japan then formally colonized Korea with the Japan-Korea Treaty of 1910. The territory was then administered by the Governor-General of Chosen, based in Keij (Seoul) until the end of the colonial period. Japan made sweeping changes in Korea. It began a process of Japanization, eventually functionally banning the use of Korean names and the Korean language altogether. It also created infrastructure and industry. Railroads, ports and roads were constructed, although in numerous cases workers were subjected to extremely poor working circumstances and discriminatory pay. While Korea's economy grew under Japan, many argue that many of the infrastructure projects were designed to extract resources from the country, and not to benefit its people. Many of the rural poor did not see the benefits of the infrastructure, and were required to send a significant amount of their agricultural output to Japan, which left many on the brink of ruin or starvation. These conditions led to the birth of the Korean Independence Movement, which acted both politically and militantly sometimes within the Japanese Empire, but mostly from outside of it. Koreans were also subjected to a number of mass murders, including the Gando Massacre, and Shinano River incident. While the international consensus is that these incidents all occurred, various Japanese scholars and politicians, including Tokyo Governor Yuriko Koike, either deny completely, attempt to justify, or downplay incidents such as these. Beginning in 1939 and during World War II, Japan began conscripting hundreds of thousands of Koreans en masse to support its war effort. Many were moved forcefully from their homes, and set to work in generally extremely poor working conditions, although there was a range in what people experienced. Some Japanese politicians and scholars, including now Prime Minister Fumio Kishida, deny that Koreans were forced laborers, and instead claim that they were "requisitioned against their will" to work. Women and girls aged 12-17 were infamously recruited, according to the international consensus, forcefully by Japan into functional sexual slavery. They are now euphemistically referred to as "comfort women", and are a continuing source of modern Japanese scholars and politicians, no tably from the far-right nationalist group Nippon Kaigi, of which Fumio Kishida and 57% of his cabinet are members of, deny that they were forced to work at all, and that even the pubescent girls consented to sex work and were compensated reasonably. After the surrender of Japan, korea was liberated, although it was immediately divided under the rule of the Soviet Union and the United States. The legacy of Japanese colonization was hotly contested even just after its end, and is still extremely controversial. There is a significant range of opinions in both South Korea and Japan, and historical topics continue to cause regular controversy. Within South Korea, a particular focus is the role of the numerous ethnic Korean collaborators ("chinilpa") with Japan, who have been variously punished or left alone. This controversy is exemplified in the legacy of Park Chung Hee, South Korea's most influential and controversial president, who collaborated with Japanese military and continued to praise it even after the colonial period. Until 1964, South Korea and Japan had no functional diplomatic relations, until they signed the Treaty on Basic Relations. Which "already null and void" the past unequal those of 1905 and 1910. Despite this, relations between Japan and South Korea have oscillated between warmer and colder periods, often due to conflicts over historiography of this era. Under the rule of military police: As Korean resistance against Japanese rule intensified, Japanese replaced Korean police system with their military police. Infamous Akashi Motojito was appointed for the commander of Japanese military police forces. Japanese finally replaced imperial Korean police forces in June 1910, and they combined police force and military police, firmly establishing the rule of annexation, Akashi started to serve as the Chief of Police. These military police officers started to have great authority over Koreans. Not only Japanese but also Koreans served as police officers. Order to change names: "you mentioned that it is necessary to grasp the people's mind, and that is true, but sometimes the higher-ups in the Governor-General's Office may have such a mindset, but it is not impossible that the lower-ranking people in the provinces and other areas may exert pressure on the people of Korea. In particular, the year before last, there was a case of changing the family name, in other words, changing the name, and the results were so good that almost 80% of the names were changed to Japanese names. I have heard some people complain that the students of the school were moved because of the pressure from the police, or that the police, or that the parents were pressured by the police. Deportation of forced labor: the combination of immigrants and forced laborers during World War II brought the brought the total to over 2 million Koreans in Japan by the end of the war, according to estimates by the Supreme Commander for the Allied Powers. In 1946, some 1,340,000 ethnic Koreans were repatriated to Korea, with 650,000 choosing to remain in Japan, where they now form the Zainichi Korean community. A 1982 survey by the Korean Youth Association showed that conscription laborers account for 13 percent of first-generation Zainichi Koreans. Japan did not draft ethnic Koreans into its military until 1944 when the tide of World War II turned against it. Until 1944, enlistment in the Imperial Japanese Army by ethnic Koreans was voluntary, and highly competitive. From a 14% acceptance rate in 1938, it dropped to a 2% acceptance rate in 1943 while the raw number of applicants increased from 3000 per annum to 300,000 in just five years during World War II. While the statistics appear to indicate that Koreans willingly joined the Japanese military, these numbers were artificially inflated using force. Japanese officials pressed illiterate peasants to sign applications and deliberately inflate statistics. This is also known in mainland Japan, and according to a 1941 survey, over half of applicants voluntarily applied due a variety of reasons, largely economic, while a small number were genuine supporters of Japan. Korea produced seven generals and numerous field grade officers (colonels, lieutenant-colonels and majors) during 35 years of colonial governance by Japan, despite institutionalized discrimination. The best-known general was Lieutenant General and Crown Prince Yi Un, who commanded Japanese forces in China and later became a member of the Supreme War Council. The other six were graduates of the Imperial Japanese Army Academy. They were: Lieutenant General Jo Seonggeun; Major General Wang Yushik; Lieutenant General Viscount Yi Beyongmu; Major General Yi Heedu; Major General Kim Eungseon (also military aide and personal guard to Prince Yi Un); and Lieutenant General Hong Sa-Ik, who was executed for war crimes committed while commanding the prison camps in the southern Philippines in 1944-1945. 574- Comfort Women: during World War II, many ethnic Korean girls and women (mostly aged 12-17) were forced by the Japanese military to become sex slaves on the pretext of being hired for jobs, such as seamstresses or factory workers, and were forced to provide sexual service for Japanese soldiers by agencies or their families against their wishes. These women were euphemistically called "comfort women". History of Korea: the Lower Paleolithic era on the Korean Peninsula and in Manchuria began roughly half a million years ago. The earliest known Korean pottery dates to around 8000 BC, and the Neolithic period began after 6000 BC, followed by the Bronze Age by 2000 BC, similarly, according to the History of Korea, the Paleolithic people are not the direct ancestors of the present Korean people, but their direct ancestors are estimated to be the Neolithic People of about 2000 BC. According to the mythic account recounted in the Gojoseon kingdom was founded in northern Korea and southern Manchuria in 2334 BC. The first written historical record on Gojoseon can be found from the text Guanzi. The Jin state was formed in southern Korea by the 3rd century BC, Gojoseon eventually fell to the Han dynasty of China, which led to succeeding warring states, the Proto-Three Kingdoms period. From the 1st century BC, Goguryeo, Baekje, and Silla grew to control the peninsula and Manchuria as the Three Kingdoms of Korea (57BC-668AD), Until unification by Silla in 676. In 698, King Go established Balhae in old territories of Goguryeo, which led to the Northern and Southern States period (698-926) of saw Balhae and Silla coexisting. In the late 9th century, Silla was divided into the Later Three Kingdoms (892-936), which ended with the unification by Wang Geon's Goryeo dynasty. Meanwhile, Balhae fell after invasions by the Khitan-Ied Liao dynasty, fleeing refugees including the last crown prince emigrated to Goryeo, where he was absorbed into the ruling family, thus unifying the two successor states of Goguryeo. During the Goryeo period, laws were codified, a civil service system was introduced, and culture influenced by Buddhism flourished. However, Mongol invasions in the 13th century brought Goryeo under the influence of the Mongol Empire and the Yuan dynasty of China until the mid-14th century. In 1392, General Yi Seong-Gye established the Joseon dynasty (1392-1897) after a coup d'etat that overthrew the Goryeo dynasty in 1388. King Sejong the Great (1418-1450) implemented numerous administrative, social, scientific, and economic reforms, established royal authority in the early years of the dynasty, and personally created Hangul, the Korean alphabet. After enjoying a period of peace for nearly two centuries, the Joseon dynasty faced foreign invasions and internal factional strife from 1592-1637. Most notable of these invasions of Korea. The combined force of the Ming dynasty of China and the Joseon dynasty repelled these Japanese invasions, but at a cost to both countries. Henceforth, Joseon gradually became more and more isolationist and stagnant. By the mid 19th century, with the country unwilling to modernize, and under encroachment by European powers, Joeson Korea was forced to sign unequal treaties with foreign powers. After the assassination of Empress M Yeongseong in 1895, the Donghak Peasant Revolution, and the Gabo Reforms of 1894 to 1896, the Korean Empire (1897-1910) came into existence, heralding a brief but rapid period of social reform and modernization. However, in 1905, the Korean Empire signed a protectorate treaty and in 1910, Japan annexed the Korean Empire.

Korea then became a Japanese colony from 1910 to 1945. Korean resistance manifested in the widespread March 1st Movement of 1919. Thereafter the resistance movements, coordinated by the Provisional Government of the Republic of Korea in exile, became largely active in neighboring Manchuria, China proper, and Siberia. After the end of World War II in 1945, the allies divided the country into a northern area (protected by the Soviets) and a southern area (protected primarily by the United States). In 1948, when the powers failed to agree on the formation of a single government, this partition became the modern states of North and South Korea. The peninsula was divided at the 38th Parallel: the "Republic of Korea" was created in the south, with the backing of the US and Western Europe, and the "Democratic People's Republic of Korea" in the north, with the backing of the Soviets and the communist People's Republic of China. The new premier of North Korea, Kim II Sung, launch the Korean War in 1950 in an attempt to reunify the country under Communist rule. After immense material and human destruction, the conflict ended with a cease-fire in 1953. In 1991, both states were accepted into the United Nations. In 2018, the two nations agreed to work toward a final settlement to formally end the Korean conflict and find the unity after ending it. While both countries were essentially under military rule after the war, South Korea eventually liberalized. Since 1987 it has had prospered, and the country is now considered to be fully developed. While North Korea has maintained a totalitarian militarized rule, with a personality cult constructed around the Kim family. Economically, North Korea has remained heavily dependent on foreign aid.

I have returned Lee Hong, Lieutenant Colonel from the South Korean battalion. We have heard the entire history of the Korean Peninsula. We have witnessed how everything slowly manifested. Now, we are going to hear experts on how to prevent conflicts and wars in the near future.

Ten ways to resolve all conflicts and end war: One- de-escalate the concept of enemy. An enemy can be reframed, in progressive order, as an adversary, competitor, partner, teacher, and finally you're equal. Two- treat the other side with respect. Otherwise, you lose them before you start. Three- recognize that there is the perception of injustice on both sides. This is a point of agreement adversaries can join in. Four- be prepared to forgive and ask for forgiveness. Here forgiveness means letting go of your desire for retribution and revenge. This is an act true courage. Even if you believe that the other side doesn't deserve forgiveness, you deserve peace. Five- refrain from belligerence. It will be taken as bullying and arouses renewed antagonism. Six- Use emotional intelligence, which means understanding the other side's feelings, giving them value, and making them equal to your feelings. Seven- reach out to understand the other side's valves, both personal and cultural. The fog of war descends when two adversaries know nothing about one another. The result is a war based on projections and prejudice. The goal is mutual acceptance. At the deepest level we all want the same things. Eight- refrain from ideological rhetoric over politics and religion. Nine- recognize that is fear on both sides. Don't be afraid to express your anxieties and to ask the other side what they are afraid of. Ten- do not insist on being right and proving the other side wrong. Give up the need to be right allows you to focus on what you actually want. Ten steps to world peace: One- start by stamping out exclusion, evidence shows that conflict happens in places where people can't trust the police or get access to justice, and their prospects for a decent life are stolen by corrupt elites. Governments everywhere need to stop the neglect, abuse and stigmatization of their own people. Media and others that promote 'them-and-us' thinking must be challenged to stop spreading hate. Two- bring about true equality between women and men, the larger a country's gender gap, the more likely it is to be involved in violent conflict, according to research in Valerie Hudson's Sex and World Peace (2012). Gender inequality trumps GDP, level of democracy or ethnic-religious identity as the strongest push factor for both external and internal conflict more likely, and being the first to resort to force in such conflicts. In contrast, when women participate in peace processes, peace is more likely to endure. Three - Share out wealth fairly, according to a World Bank survey, 40 per cent of those who join rebel groups do so because of a lack of economic opportunities. Relative poverty is just as important, with more equal societies marked by high levels of trust and low levels of violence. Economic fairness when it comes to public resources, taxation and tax evasion is also key. The systematic transfer of wealth from rich to poor-instead of the other way round-improves security for everyone. Four- tackle climate change, ecological stress from global warming is proven to exacerbate conflicts over resources such as land and water, particularly in East Africa. For all its shortcomings, the UN climate agreement is evidence that the world can tackle and mitigate crises by co-operation, instead of war. A functioning climate deal 'is the greatest peace deal the world could have', according to Dan Smith, from the leading arms-control think tank SIPRI. Five- control arm sales, the promotion of arms sales and heavy spending on aggressive military capabilities is heightening global tensions. The proliferation of arms drives conflict and makes violence more likely. Arms treaty signatories makes violence more likely. Arms treaty signatories must be held to their word, as we build evidence of violations and hold sellers accountable. We can also build support for a groundbreaking new convention that bans nuclear weapons and makes it illegal to possess or use them. Six- Display less hubris, make more policy change, a look at the track record of counter-terrorism, the 'war on drugs', stabilization and state-building efforts and colonial wars 'shows a pattern of largely very sobering failure 'says Saferworlds's Larry Attree. Humanity and willingness to atone for past aggression on the international stage is essential-as is an end to the self-serving and counter-productive policy in the Middle-East. Seven- protect political space, if young, marginalized people to embrace an open society rather than pursue more violent and vengeful paths, they must allow public dissent. Across the world-and the political spectrum-this space must be defended from repressive tools such as ad hoc administrative regulation, misuse of anti-terrorist measures, arbitrary arrest and imprisonment, even torture and murder. Eight-fix intergenerational relations, much conflict can be understood as a youth revolt against established corrupt systems run by, generally, older men. In countries with strict age hierarchies young people can't voice their frustrations, which creates a dangerous dynamic, explains researcher and peacebuilder Chitra Nagarajan. This is compounded by classic victim-blaming. In which young men are treated as a ticking time bomb. Nine- build an integrated peace movement, short-term anti-war movements have taken the the place of active and permanent peace movements. We need to promote nonviolent alternatives and successes; peace campaigner Phyllis Bennis believes peace must be woven into other social movements, giving the example of the Poor People's Campaign in the US last March, which attacked the war economy and linked it to poverty at home. Ten- look within, peace starts with you. Ordinary, citizens can make a difference. When's the last time you said sorry? Think about who loses when you win. Are the people around you heard and respected or marginalized, ignored and left out? Make a decision to care about what happens to them. Start a constructive conversation with someone you disagree with. Challenge 'them-and-us' thinking in yourself as well as in others. Everyone of us can choose to make society more just and peaceful, or more unjust and warlike. Impact of wars on the evolution of civilizations: abstract, throughout the evolutionary track of human, the evolution or extinction of both ancient and modern civilizations are characterized by processes like growth, assimilation, invasion, aggression, and annihilation.

How did human civilizations evolve through wars and assimilations as envisaged in history? Introduction: the gloom and glory of war and the eventual rise and fall of human civilization has fascinated all of our ancient and modern history. Ethnicity, religion, politics, nationalism, racism, humiliation, glamor, or whatever the main driving factors for triggering a war, their violent impact had drastically changed (damaged or improved) the growth, development, culture, economy, and technology of human civilizations. Self-immolation and power of resilience are reckoned as the striking characteristics in the history of civilization starting from its very beginning is dynamic in nature as it changes constantly in the passage of time until it has perished. How did human civilizations evolve through wars and assimilations as envisaged in history? Concluding remarks: war is a global and a historical phenomena, closely interwoven with the conquest and destruction of human civilizations. Although traditional warfare or wars of the European expansion obey different logics than the great power wars of the eighteenth and nineteenth centuries, one of the main causes of triggering a war is the extension of territory. This is reflected in our simple domain growth based toy model and, as such, analogies can be.

Future wars-and how prevent them: the world is entering a new era of warfare, with cyber and autonomous weapons taking center stage. These technologies are making militaries faster, smarter, more efficient. But if unchecked, they threaten to destabilize the world. DW takes a deep dive into the future of conflict, uncovering an even more volatile world. Where cyber intrusion against a nuclear early warning system can unleash a terrifying spiral of escalation; where "flash wars" can erupt from autonomous weapons interacting so fast that no human could keep up. Germany's Foreign Minister Heiko Maas tells DW that we have already entered the technological arms race that is propelling us towards this future, "we're right in the middle of it, that's the reality the reality we have to deal with". And yet the world is failing to meet the challenge. Talks on controlling autonomous weapons have repeatedly been stalled by major powers seeking to carve out their own advantage. And cyber conflict has become not just a fear of the future but a permanent state of affairs. DW finds out what must happen to steer the world in a safer direction, with leading voices from the world's of politics, diplomacy, intelligence, academia, and activism speaking out.

Final conclusion from Lieutenant Colonel Lee Hong, from the South Korean battalion. My observation after witnessing and participating in an actual endless war. After hearing all the heartbreaking testimonies, hearing about the entire history of the Korean Peninsula, how everything manifested. After hearing the so called experts describe how wars and conflicts can be prevented. These are my personal conclusions. Human egos are the worst thing ever, if you take away the human egos, life on our planet would be so much better. My observation is seeing the exact opposite of what nations are doing. The mind set is if you build a strong military with major capabilities no one on earth would dare to invade you. Something else that is happening is no nation trusts each other. The hunger for nuclear weapons and other advanced technologies are greater than ever. I see leaders of nations deciding how our world should be, like gods. I see ignorance from humanity in addressing other nations concerns. I see no efforts in coordinating real conclusive results on solving major problems that are destroying our precious planet. I see no respect for the beauty of our world and try to work together to conserve it. Exploiting resources and just taking everything, the differences in ideologies is also none beneficial. True peace is when no matter who they are can figure out how to solve differences in a peaceful way without being so primitive as using might and power over intelligence and coordination.